aliens
to earth

aliens
to earth

stories chosen by
wendy cooling

Dolphin

A Dolphin Paperback

First published in Great Britain in 1997
by Orion Children's Books
a division of the Orion Publishing Group Ltd
Orion House
5 Upper St Martin's Lane
London WC2H 9EA

A catalogue record for this book is available from the British Library
Typeset by Deltatype Ltd, Birkenhead, Merseyside
Printed in Great Britain by Clays Ltd, St Ives plc
ISBN 1 85881 443 X

contents

mel and squid and the dustbin from space

douglas hill

The cat was lost – again. So Mel had to search for him, on a Saturday morning bright with autumn sunshine, when there were a *million* better things to do. And that meant starting in the back lane, among all the weeds and clutter and smelly dustbins.

But there were no cats at all to be seen in the lane, even after Mel – short for Melanie – had jogged up and down its length twice, calling. She was a leggy eleven-year-old, trim in jeans and sweatshirt, with short dark hair and a normally happy face. But there in the lane she was scowling with annoyance, wasting her day searching for a silly cat. And she was still scowling when she looked around and saw a red-haired boy idling along the lane towards her.

'Squid!' Mel called. 'Have you seen Dan?'

The boy stopped, considering the question. He was a neighbour from a few houses away – some months younger than Mel, not yet quite eleven, shorter and tubbier, with a round face and round glasses, also wearing jeans with a scruffy shirt. His real name was Arthur, but he was called Squid because of a mishap he had once had with some seafood.

'You shouldn't have called your cat Dan Dare,' Squid said, grinning. 'It makes him think he has to have adventures.'

Mel's scowl deepened. Squid could be a bit of a comedian, which was all right if you were in the mood. But she wasn't. 'I don't think he's in outer space,' she said shortly. 'Have you *seen* him?'

The boy nodded. 'He was around here just a few minutes ago ...'

Almost as if in reply to those words, they both heard a faint mewing sound. It seemed to come from a cluster of four metal dustbins, standing next to one of the nearby garden gates.

Hurrying over, they saw no sign of the cat. But then Mel moved the newest and shiniest bin aside – and there was Dan Dare, crouching over a discarded scrap of food.

'What are you *doing* there?' Mel said, picking the cat up.

And then she and Squid went stiff with astonishment. Because, from somewhere next to them, a breathy high-pitched voice replied.

'I'm here because I'm *stuck*!' the voice cried. 'And I need help!'

'Who said that?' Squid said, spinning around.

'I did!' the voice said. 'I'm the ...' It paused as if looking for a word. 'The metal container that you just moved!'

'Very funny,' Mel said, peering over the gate into the garden. 'A talking dustbin ... Come out, right now, wherever you are ...'

'I wish I *could*,' the voice said wistfully. 'But that's the trouble. I'm not a dustbin, I just *look* like one at the moment. And I wish I didn't ...'

Mel and Squid stared. The shiny dustbin looked perfectly ordinary, and when Squid warily lifted its lid it was perfectly empty. It couldn't *possibly* be speaking. And yet – there was no one else ...

But in that moment, someone else did speak, making them both jump. It was a sour-looking old man with a cane, hobbling out of the house that went with the garden, the gate and the dustbins. His name was Grinton, known as 'Grumpy' to the local children, because he was usually as ill-natured as he looked.

'You two!' the old man shouted, waving his walking stick. 'What are you doing? Get away from there!'

'Just getting my cat, Mr Grinton,' Mel said, holding up Dan Dare.

'Well, you got it,' the old man snapped. 'So clear off!'

Glowering, Mel and Squid moved slowly away. But when the old man had hobbled back into his house, and when Mel had let Dan Dare go, they ducked down behind the fence and crept back to stare at the shiny dustbin.

'Did we really hear that voice?' Mel muttered. 'Or were we dreaming?'

'No, I really did speak to you,' the voice said. 'And I'm really in trouble. I'm from another world ...'

'An alien visitor!' Squid said, his eyes shining. 'Where's your spaceship?'

'That's the trouble,' the voice said. 'You see, on my world people can *change shape*, to turn into all sorts of different things. So we don't *ride* spaceships – we turn ourselves *into* ships, to travel in space.'

Mel laughed. 'Squid, are you throwing your voice or something?'

'I'm not doing anything,' Squid said, sounding awed. 'And there's nobody else here. It's really happening, Mel – an alien ...'

'Anyway,' the breathy voice went on, 'I wanted to land here last night for a look around, but I came in too fast and didn't see the fence in time. So I crashed and knocked myself out – and when I came to, I was in this dustbin shape! And I can't change back to a ship or anything else! I'm *stuck* like this – and I don't know what to do!'

The voice trembled as if on the verge of tears, but Mel was too amazed to notice. While the voice had gone on speaking, Squid had put a hand over his mouth, to prove he wasn't doing it. And if he wasn't – then it might be true ...

'You know, Mel,' Squid said, taking his hand away, 'old Grumpy Grinton only had *three* dustbins, here in the lane, before.'

'That's right,' the strange voice said. 'There were three when I got here.'

Mel shook her head, feeling dazed. 'Do you *believe*

this, Squid? A talking dustbin that's really an alien being?'

'If I could change shape, I'd prove it,' the voice said mournfully. 'Maybe if you help me I'll be able to change again, and show you.'

'Help you how?' Squid asked.

The voice was silent for a moment, again as if pondering. 'You could try *moving* me,' it said at last. 'Being next to these other bins might be helping to keep me in this shape.'

'Right,' Squid said firmly. 'Come on, Mel.'

'Just hope Grumpy Grinton isn't watching,' Mel said. But she and Squid readily took the dustbin's handles, to move it away from the other bins.

The voice sighed. 'It's very kind of you … And your names are Mel and Squid? That's nice and easy … I don't think you could even *say* my name.'

Squid smiled. 'Then we'll call you Bin, for now.'

Mel was still feeling dazed and doubtful, and a bit silly to be talking to a dustbin. But then they put it – him – down in the middle of the lane. And saw that everything he had said was true.

The dustbin, Bin, seemed to quiver and grow suddenly hazy and blurred. For an instant Mel and Squid saw the shadowy form of a small man with a hairless pointy head and blueish skin, wearing a shiny sort of coverall.

Then the strange image was gone – and Bin was a dustbin again.

'It's no good,' Bin said miserably in his breathy voice. 'I'm still stuck in this shape.'

Mel took a big shaky breath. 'Do you know *why* you're stuck?' she asked.

'Because of the crash,' Bin said. 'It must have knocked something out of kilter in my systems.'

Squid nodded wisely. 'The way a bash on the head can make someone lose their memory ... You've lost the shape-changing *knack*, Bin.'

'But you did change, after you crashed,' Mel said, puzzled. 'Into a bin.'

'I think that was sort of automatic,' Bin said. 'While I was knocked out, and lying in among those other dustbins.'

Mel nibbled her lip, thinking. 'Then what if we took you and put you down somewhere with a lot of *other* things? You might automatically change into one of *them*!'

'Good one, Mel!' Squid said excitedly. 'That might give you back the knack, Bin – so after that you could charge into a spaceship again!'

'We could try,' Bin said, sounding a little more hopeful. 'And – it might be an idea to put me among things that can *fly*. I might manage the change to a spaceship more easily up in the air.'

So Mel and Squid set off, lugging the dustbin out of the lane and along the street, looking for flying things that might help Bin to change shape.

But they had no luck at all.

They tried several times to set Bin down among groups of pigeons gathered on the pavement, but the birds always flew away at once. So did sparrows in a bush and starlings on a lawn. They tried to sneak Bin into a pet shop to put him beside the bird cages, but the shopkeeper ordered them out. Mel had the idea of trying a kite shop, and Squid thought of a model aeroplane shop, but the same thing happened. No one would let them bring a dustbin into a shop.

Also, while they were trudging along carrying the shiny dustbin, they were getting a great many curious or amused looks, and some laughter, from people on the street. So Mel and Squid were growing more and more red-faced and embarrassed. And it was even more embarrassing when, now and then, along the way, Bin kept trying to change his shape.

Once, as they went past a supermarket, he went into his quivering haziness again as if trying to change into a shopping trolley. He failed, and snapped back to his dustbin shape at once, but he left a crowd of shoppers looking startled and troubled. In the same way, over the next while, Bin tried at different times to change into a cardboard box, a poodle, a parking meter, an oak tree, and a baby's pram with a baby in it. Each time he failed, still stuck in the dustbin shape – and each time Mel and Squid had to flee from baffled and upset onlookers.

'We're not getting anywhere,' Mel said at last. 'And if we keep on, we could be arrested or something.'

'What about taking him to the airport?' Squid suggested. 'He could try turning into a plane.'

Mel frowned. 'I'm not sure how to get there. And they probably wouldn't let us in anyway, with Bin.'

'I suppose,' Squid sighed. 'But we have to think of something ...'

'I'm sorry, Mel and Squid,' Bin said unhappily. 'Maybe there's nothing anyone can do. Maybe I'll have to be a dustbin forever ...'

He sounded as if he was about to cry, again, and Mel was just about to say something soothing, when she saw what seemed to be the perfect solution.

They had wandered through the town in sort of a circle, and had come to the edge of a small park near their homes. By the park entrance, things were being sold, as usual, from carts or vans – ice cream, hot dogs and so on. But one man, standing alone, had something different for sale.

Balloons.

'Squid!' Mel cried, pointing. 'If Bin could change into a balloon, he could float up ...'

'I may not be able to,' Bin said glumly.

'We can try,' Squid said. And then he went still, struck with a new idea. 'Mel – you know that old tree house I made, in my garden? If we got him up there, away from everything, where no one can see ...'

'With balloons!' Mel cried. 'Good idea!'

They rushed excitedly to the balloon man, who politely tried not to stare at the dustbin they were carrying. Their pocket money was enough to buy five balloons, which the man filled for them. And then they dashed away as fast as they could, with Bin, back to Squid's house.

But because they went along the lane again, to get into Squid's garden through the back gate, they were spotted.

'Ah-ha!' cried Grumpy Grinton, standing at his garden gate, waving his stick. 'Caught you! Thought I wouldn't see you before, stealing my bin!'

Squid looked a bit scared, but Mel scowled at the old man. 'This bin isn't yours, Mr Grinton! You had three bins, and you *still* have three!'

The old man looked around at the three bins by his gate. 'Oh, no,' he said nastily. 'You've stolen that nice clean bin from me and left me some dirty old one in its place! I'm calling the *police*, I am!'

As he hobbled swiftly away towards the back door, muttering, Mel looked at Squid, then gave Bin a little shake. 'You'd better turn into something else soon,' she said. 'Or we're in trouble.'

They hurried into Squid's garden, hoping that no one was watching from a window as they dashed over to the big tree that held the tree house. It was really just an uneven platform of boards with an old blanket for a roof, and smaller boards nailed to the tree trunk like steps of a ladder. Squid scrambled up to lower a frayed old rope that Mel tied to one of Bin's handles.

Then she climbed up, carefully taking the balloons, to help Squid pull Bin up.

Another time Mel would have enjoyed being up in the big tree, with the sun filtering through the leaves in their autumn colours, which fluttered in the breeze that gently rocked the branches. But just then she and Squid had more important things to think about. Especially when, after they put the balloons all around Bin, nothing happened.

Bin tried his best, going hazy and blurry again. For a second, he did manage to look like a many-coloured little balloon – and for another instant he looked like a strange little flying machine, with a wide flat metal body and stubby wings. But neither shape became solid, and at once he was a dustbin again.

'Oh, Bin …' Mel said unhappily.

Bin sighed. 'My shape-changing ability must *really* have been damaged, in the crash …' He paused, pondering, while Mel and Squid looked at each other hopelessly. 'I know,' Bin went on. 'Let's try tying balloons to my handles, and then *dropping* me … Falling through the air, not standing on anything, might help me to change into a balloon.'

'Falling?' Mel repeated worriedly. 'You could be hurt!'

'What does it matter?' Bin asked gloomily. 'I'm damaged already.'

'Sometimes,' Squid said, 'people who've lost their

memory from a bash on the head get it *back* with another bash.'

'Right!' Bin said. 'Let's try it!'

So they did as he asked – tying the balloons to his handles, taking him to the edge of the platform, then nervously, hesitantly, dropping him.

It might have been a comical sight – a shiny dustbin decorated with balloons falling out of a tree. But Mel and Squid weren't laughing. They simply stared down anxiously as Bin fell. He bounced against a branch or two on the way, and some of the balloons burst among the twigs. And then Bin crashed to the ground with a loud *clang*, and lay unmoving in a heap of dry fallen leaves – still in his dustbin form, entirely unchanged.

'Bin?' Mel called down anxiously. 'Are you all right?'

'I'm fine, I think,' Bin said, his voice muffled by the leaves. 'Though I feel a bit funny, inside. And … it didn't work.'

But then, before Mel and Squid could say or do anything more, three startling things happened, one after another.

First, a powerful gust of autumn wind whipped up the dry leaves from the ground, pulling others from the big tree to join them in a swirling blizzard of yellow and brown.

Second, a woman's voice shouted '*Arthur!*' – and Mel, surprised to hear Squid's real name, saw his mother marching angrily towards them from the house. Followed by a tall, helmeted policeman.

And third – as Mel and Squid began to feel a clenching of alarm – Bin suddenly disappeared.

The two of them stared down open-mouthed at where Bin had lain, before shifting their gaze to stare at the approaching adults. And then a large, bright yellow leaf came swooping towards them, as if carried by the wind, settling on to the tree house next to Mel's foot.

'Look!' the leaf said, in a tiny breathy voice that sounded exactly like Bin's. 'I changed shape!'

'Bin?' Mel gasped. 'Is that *you*?'

'Who else?' the leaf cried merrily. 'Crashing to the ground like that must have jolted my systems back into action, just as Squid said! When the wind blew the leaves into the air, I just changed and went with them …'

As Mel and Squid began to smile with delight, Squid's mother and the policeman arrived at the foot of the tree.

'Melanie?' she said. 'I thought that was you … What have you two been doing? Mr Grinton reported you to the *police*!'

The policeman gazed up sternly. 'You kids had better come down while we sort this out. Mr Grinton claims you stole one of his dustbins.'

Squid and Mel put on wide-eyed, innocent expressions. 'A *dustbin*? Us?' Squid asked. 'Why would he think that?' Mel asked.

'Good question,' the policeman said. 'But come on down.'

'I'd better be going,' Bin whispered in his small leaf-voice. 'If the wind carries me high enough, I can take my spaceship form without being seen. So I'll say goodbye, now – and I can't thank you enough for your help. I'd have been stuck for ever, without you, and I won't ever forget you. I just hope I haven't got you into trouble.'

'I wish you didn't have to go so soon,' Mel murmured sadly, feeling more upset about Bin leaving than about facing the policeman.

'Could you come back some time to see us?' Squid whispered, just as sadly.

'Maybe,' Bin said. As he spoke, a new gust of wind rushed past, snatching him up into the air. ''Bye, Mel and Squid!' he said in his tiny voice as he was swirled away. ''Bye!'

''Bye, Bin,' Mel said softly, and Squid moved a hand in a small wave.

'Are you coming down?' his mother called up impatiently.

'Right away,' Squid said, going to the ladder. 'But we don't have any dustbins up here, I promise you that.'

'Or anywhere else,' Mel added, glancing up at the

big yellow leaf that was flying higher and higher into the sky.

'I'm glad to hear it,' the policeman said. 'I expect Mr Grinton has got a bit muddled, somehow.'

Mel and Squid started down, still gazing at the sky as they did so. The leaf that was Bin was just a tiny dot in the sky by then – and as they gazed they saw the dot suddenly disappear. In its place they saw a small flying machine, with a wide flat body and stubby wings, which flashed away, up and up, at terrific speed, to be lost to sight in a moment.

And the two adults had noticed nothing at all.

'That must be it,' Squid's mother said briskly. 'The old fellow is confused. After all – what on *earth* would two children want with someone's dustbin?'

Mel and Squid grinned at each other as they reached the ground.

'Nothing on *earth*,' Mel whispered. 'Nothing on Earth, at all.'

the boy from
the back
of beyond

helen johnson

Lyall's mum sent him to wash his hands before dinner. Lyall stomped out of the caravan and ran across the muddy site with a towel over his head. It was still raining. It had been raining every day for the past four days. Caravan holiday weather, Dad called it.

There was nobody else in the men's shower block. Lyall turned the tap on and pulled faces at himself in the mirror while he waited for the warm water to come through. Then he heard a noise.

'Pssst!' said a voice.

Lyall dropped the soap into the basin and turned round. He couldn't see anybody.

The noise came again. 'Pssst!'

Then Lyall noticed a pair of eyes looking at him from above one of the shower curtains – which was strange because he couldn't see any feet underneath the curtain.

'Help me! I'm stuck!' said the voice.

Lyall walked over to the cubicle, wiping his hands on his trousers. He pulled open the curtain and blinked. Hard.

The person – it was impossible to say whether it was a boy or a man – was standing on the wall, about level with Lyall's head. He was wearing huge blue shorts and a white T-shirt with 'DONT ASK ME – I'M NEW

HERE!' printed across the front. His feet, encased in butter-yellow boots, were planted firmly on the tiles and his body was completely horizontal.

'Wow! How do you do that?' asked Lyall. 'How did you get up there?'

'I thought it was the ground,' said the person.

Lyall frowned. 'But what's holding you up there? Why aren't you falling down?'

'It's my boots,' whispered the person.

'Your boots!' exclaimed Lyall.

'Sssshh!' The person peered round the edge of the cubicle to make sure nobody was listening. 'Please do not speak about the boots!'

'But …?'

'Questions, questions! Please help me down. This sideways is making me feel unwell.' The person held out his hand and Lyall took it. The person *was* beginning to look very pale. Perhaps it would be better to save his questions until later.

Slowly, the person lifted one foot and began to walk down the wall. When he reached the ground he righted himself and smoothed down his shorts. Then he grinned up at Lyall. He was very short – at least six inches shorter than Lyall – and he had a young-looking face. But his hair was sparse and wispy and his hand was wrinkly like an old man's hand. Lyall couldn't begin to guess what sort of age he was. He could have been anything from six to sixty.

'Thank you. You are my best friend! I am Oran,' said the person, shaking Lyall's hand.

'That's okay,' said Lyall. 'I'm Lyall. But how …?'

'Is this Holiday?' whispered Oran, looking round at the basins and shower cubicles.

'This room isn't holiday,' said Lyall. 'We're on holiday.'

Oran pointed at the blue and white tiles beneath his yellow boots. 'Is that Holiday?'

'No!' laughed Lyall. 'A holiday isn't a thing! It's something you go on.'

'Like a bus?'

'No. Not like a bus.' Lyall frowned. It was difficult to explain. 'It's when you go somewhere to enjoy yourself.'

'A party? The funfair?'

'No!' said Lyall again. 'It's like … a break.'

Oran frowned. 'A break? Snap? Kaput?'

'Not that sort of break. A rest sort of break.'

Oran nodded. 'Rest sort of break. Enjoy yourself. Excuse me one moment.' He dipped his thin wrinkly hand into the pocket of his baggy shorts and pulled out a notebook and pencil. He wrote something down.

'Only it's better when it's not raining,' said Lyall.

'Raining?' said Oran.

'You know – drip. Water from the sky?'

'Ah! Rain!' said Oran, making another note in his book. Then he snapped the book shut and smiled.

'Good! So now I am in the right place. And the right way up! I will have holiday with you!'

'Hmmm, maybe,' said Lyall, cautiously. 'How come you haven't heard of a holiday before?'

'We don't have them where I come from,' said Oran.

'Where's that?' asked Lyall. He thought everybody had heard of holidays, even if they never had one themselves.

'Oh – The Back of Beyond,' said Oran, waving his skinny arm.

Lyall had never heard of The Back of Beyond.

'Where's that? Is that where you got your boots from? Is it far from here?'

Oran suddenly looked sad. 'It is a very long way and I do not want to talk about it.'

Lyall thought Oran must be homesick. He would have to try to be friendly and not mention The Back of Beyond again.

Suddenly Oran gasped.

'Oh no! It is raining in here!' he said, pointing towards the basin.

The soap had blocked the plughole. Water was dripping over the side of the basin and splashing onto the floor.

'That's not rain! It's just tapwater overflowing,' said Lyall. 'It's made a bit of a puddle though!' He turned off the tap and pulled the soap out of the basin. 'I'd better go now,' he said. 'My dinner's ready.'

'Goodbye!' called Oran. 'We will bump together again, no doubt!'

It was still raining the next morning. Lyall and his mum and dad went to the tiny museum in the town. It was very dull and dusty. Lyall gazed up at the cobwebby ceiling and wondered if Oran could walk across ceilings too, like a fly. Then he bumped into somebody.

'Sorry! Oh – it's you!' said Lyall, recognising the butter-yellow boots.

Oran picked himself off the floor and dusted down his blue shorts. 'Hello, friend! Don't worry. No harm done!'

Oran grinned up at Lyall and his parents.

'This is Oran,' explained Lyall. 'I met him at the caravan site yesterday.'

'Lyall is my friend,' beamed Oran. 'He has been most helpful to me.' Oran held out his hand and Lyall's dad shook it.

Lyall's dad was very impressed with Oran's manners. 'Well, why don't we two go off and leave you together?' he said.

'Yes,' agreed Lyall's mum, who was happy that Lyall had made such a nice friend. 'There's no point in you trailing around with us. We'll see you later. Have fun!'

'Okay,' said Lyall, grinning at Oran. Now he wouldn't have to look at the boring fossils. Oran grinned back. He looked around at the bits of boats, and the curling posters on the walls, and the broken model lighthouse with a light that didn't work. A badly stuffed seagull with a broken beak dangled from the ceiling on a piece of blue washing-line.

'So this is where you go on holiday?' said Oran. 'To enjoy yourself?'

'Not really,' said Lyall. 'But we can't go on the beach until stops raining. Holidays aren't much fun if the sun never shines.'

'Wait! I must write this down,' said Oran. He produced the notebook and pencil from his shorts pocket and turned over a page.

'Why do you want to know about holidays?' asked Lyall.

'It is my homework,' said Oran.

Lyall nodded. He had had to write about his holiday the year before.

'Tell me more,' said Oran.

Lyall tried to explain. 'Holiday is when you go and stay somewhere else. You have fun and games and you don't have to go to school or work. You can stay in bed in the mornings.'

'Bed? Where is your holiday bed?'

'In the caravan,' said Lyall. 'We sleep in sleeping bags.'

'So you sleep in a bag in the metal box on wheels?' said Oran. 'And in the day, you come to museums?'

Lyall sighed. 'Only because of the rain. It's been raining cats and dogs all week.'

'Cats and dogs?' Oran looked up at the tall windows and frowned.

'Not *real* cats and dogs!' said Lyall. 'It's just a joke.'

'Oh,' said Oran, who didn't think it was a very funny joke.

'I wish it was sunny,' said Lyall. 'I want to go on the beach. The beach is brilliant – sun and sea and tons of sand to play on.'

'I would like to see Beach,' said Oran. He stood up and put the notebook away. 'I must go now. There is much work to do. Thank you for your help.' He shook Lyall's hand. 'It will be sunny tomorrow and we will go to the beach.'

Lyall didn't believe him.

But it *was* sunny the next day. Suddenly the caravan site came to life. Bags full of grass mats and beach balls and windbreaks appeared outside each door. Picnics were packed and swimsuits put on. The shop ran out of suntan cream and size five flip-flops. By eleven o'clock the site was almost deserted as everybody made their way down the sandy cliff path to the beach.

Lyall was hardly surprised at all when he tripped over a small figure bending down to tie his shoelaces. It was Oran, of course.

'Hello, friend!' said Oran, falling into step beside his friend. 'Is this to the beach?'

'Yes,' said Lyall. 'Look! There it is!'

He pointed down at the bright sand and dazzling sea.

'Oh!' gasped Oran. 'It is a big puddle!'

'That's not a puddle – that's the sea!'

'But the sea is wet? You didn't like the wet.'

'I didn't like the wet when it was coming down as rain. It's different when it's the sea.'

Oran didn't look convinced.

'Come on!' yelled Lyall. 'I'll race you down!'

At the foot of the path, Lyall sat down and tugged off his trainers. 'You'd better take your boots off – the water will ruin them,' he said.

'I will stay on the beach,' said Oran, 'and make notes.'

'Please yourself,' said Lyall. 'Last one in the water's a monkey's uncle!' he shouted, and ran off down the beach.

Monkey's uncle? Oran shook his head and trotted after his friend. This boy said a lot of strange things!

Oran stood on the sand and made notes while his friend swam. This water was interesting. It wasn't flat like the water in the basin. It had hills and ridges, and it moved. Oran noticed that every so often the water came nearer, and he kept having to walk a bit further up the beach. The water was growing!

At last, Lyall came out of the water. 'Come on! I'm starving. Let's go and get something to eat. How about a hot dog?'

'A hot dog?' said Oran. He looked at a golden

labrador which lay panting in the shade of a beach umbrella. Oran looked horrified. 'I thought that human ... err ... people loved dogs. I didn't know you ate them.' Oran patted the dog's head. 'Poor thing,' he said. 'Such a sad ending.'

'I'm not going to eat a *real* dog!' laughed Lyall. 'A hot dog is a sausage in a roll.'

'A sausage dog?'

'No! It's ... well, it's a sort of joke.'

'Ah, another joke,' nodded Oran. He had heard that jokes were complicated and difficult to understand, and that was proving to be the case. He made a note in his book. 'I would like to try this joke food,' said Oran.

As they walked back up the beach, Oran confided, 'I don't wish to alarm you, Lyall, but the sea is growing. I think it may overflow – like the basin. It nearly swallowed my shoes back there.'

'The sea can't overflow,' said Lyall. 'It just moves up and down a bit – it's called the tide. It's something to do with the moon's gravity. It's like a sort of magnet.'

'I know gravity,' said Oran.

Lyall thought about Oran's wall-walking. He looked down at the yellow boots. 'You see that cliff? I bet if you wanted to, you could climb right up there.'

Oran looked up. 'It is possible,' he said.

'Then why don't you? It would be fun,' said Lyall.

'I think it would cause trouble,' said Oran. 'Somebody might see me.'

'That wouldn't matter,' said Lyall.

'But they would find out about my boots!' said Oran. 'Nobody must know. They are secret.'

'You mean like when somebody invents something, and they patent it so nobody else can copy it?'

Oran nodded. 'You mustn't tell anybody.'

'Okay. Your secret's safe with me,' said Lyall. 'I wish you'd let me have a go, though.'

'I don't think it would be a good idea,' said Oran, snapping his notebook shut. 'Can we have hot dogs now?'

Oran decided that hot dogs were his favourite sort of food. He ate three of them. He was glad they weren't made of real dog.

After lunch, Lyall said they should dig down to Australia.

Oran frowned. 'Lyall, it is twelve-thousand-seven-hundred-and-fourteen kilometres from one side of the world to the other. Which means that one boy, using a standard plastic beach spade, and not stopping for lunch, would take approximately …' Oran's fingers began to work, 'seventy-two years, six months and twenty-eight days to dig that far. Besides, the centre of the earth is far too hot. Your spade would melt.'

'I know all that!' said Lyall. 'It's just a joke.'

'Like hot dogs? And monkey's uncle?'

'That sort of thing,' said Lyall.

Oran and Lyall dug quite a big hole, but got tired

before they were anywhere near Australia. So then they built a huge sandcastle with all the sand they'd dug out of the hole. They dug a channel all the way up the beach to a moat, and then they sat and waited until the tide came right in and flooded it.

It was sunny again the next day. Oran came round to the caravan and Lyall suggested a game of football. Oran had never heard of football, so Lyall fetched his ball from under the caravan and showed Oran how to kick.

'Now you try,' said Lyall, tapping the ball to Oran. Oran pulled back his butter-yellow boot and aimed his right foot at the ball. Then he kicked it – hard. The ball flew into the air, growing smaller and smaller until it was just a tiny speck in the sky.

'Wow!' said Lyall. Maybe Oran's boots were all-round magic boots. It was a stunning kick for somebody who hadn't even heard of football. And where on earth had nobody heard of football?

At last, the ball reached its peak and began to come down again. Oran and Lyall watched it as it fell, faster and faster, closer and closer … until it disappeared over the swimming pool wall. There was a big splash.

The gate to the swimming pool was locked.

'We will have to wait until morning,' said Oran.

'Why don't we get it now?' suggested Lyall. 'You could walk over this wall.'

Oran looked doubtful.

'Nobody will see you,' said Lyall. 'And you

wouldn't need to get your boots wet. There's a big pole on the wall for fishing things out of the water. Go on – I'll keep watch.'

Oran looked around. There was nobody about.

'All right,' he said, reluctantly. 'Just this once.'

He tucked his T-shirt into his shorts, wriggled his toes, and set off up the wall. Lyall watched him disappear over the top and heard his footsteps coming down the other side. A little later, Oran whispered, 'I have got it.' The footsteps came up the wall again and Oran appeared with the ball under his arm. He handed it to Lyall.

'Thanks!' said Lyall. 'I wish I could do that!'

Oran shrugged. 'It is nothing,' he said.

The sun shone for the rest of the week. Lyall and Oran spent every day on the beach digging holes to Australia, and playing football. Lyall got better at football and Oran got better at digging. Lyall offered to teach Oran to swim, but Oran refused to take off his boots.

Soon it was the last evening of the holiday. Lyall's dad cooked sausages on the barbecue and Oran and Lyall sat on the grass eating hot dogs. Then Oran told Lyall his news.

'I have finished my homework. Tonight, I have to go back.'

'To The Back of Beyond?'

'Yes,' said Oran.

Lyall fiddled with a few blades of grass. He didn't

want Oran to go home. His holiday had been much more fun with him around. And much sunnier.

'Perhaps we could write to each other,' said Lyall.

'I'm afraid we don't have a very good postal service in The Back of Beyond,' said Oran. 'But please give me your address. You have been a good friend to me. I would like to send you a present. What would you like?'

Lyall thought. There were lots of things he wanted. A leather football, a high bed with a ladder, a computer game, one of those massive bars of chocolate ... But it was easy to choose.

'What I would like most of all is – a special pair of boots like yours,' said Lyall.

Oran looked down and wriggled his toes. 'This is difficult. These boots were specially made for me and my ... circumstances,' said Oran. 'They might not suit you.'

'Well, I admit that yellow isn't the colour I would have chosen,' agreed Lyall. 'But I'm not fussy. Any colour would do.' He lay down on the grass and folded his arms behind his head. 'If I had boots like that, I'd walk up walls all the time.'

Oran sighed. He wouldn't like his friend to get into trouble. He looked up at the clear black sky, where millions of stars were blinking and sparkling like glitter on black cardboard.

'I will send you some special boots,' Oran promised.

'Boots specially made for you and your ... circumstances.'

'Thanks!' said Lyall.

'Now I must go,' said Oran. He shook Lyall's hand and stood up. 'Goodbye, friend.'

When Lyall woke up the next day it was raining again. He looked out of the caravan window and wondered where Oran was now. He hoped he'd got back safely to The Back of Beyond. He wondered if it was raining there.

It rained all the way home. When they got back there was a parcel waiting on the doorstep. The boots! Lyall carried the box indoors. There was an envelope taped to the top. Lyall tried to read the postmark but it was smudged. He opened the letter.

'Dear Lyall,' it said.

'Thank you for helping me with my homework. I have explained to my fellows about holidays, and fun and games, and the big puddle on the beach. I have told them about jokes too, but I don't think they understand. Jokes are difficult.

'I think holiday is just doing something different. Although I have been working, I have had a holiday. Thank you.

'It would be nice if you could have a holiday and come to The Back of Beyond, but I fear it is too far, and you would not be able to walk properly on our ground because it is sideways.'

Lyall paused. How could ground be sideways? He read on.

'Here are the special boots I promised you. They aren't exactly like mine. Now that I am not there with you, there may be rather a lot of rain for a while. The water has to fall sometime so I have made your boots waterproof. Also, you said that you didn't like yellow very much, so yours are a different colour. I hope you will like these. Remember to be sensible with them. Wall-walking can be very dangerous. And please remember that nobody must ever find out about them. May we bump together in the future.

Your friend,

Oran.'

Lyall ripped open the box. Inside was a special pair of boots – a very special pair of boots.

Lyall lifted them out. They were glossy navy-blue and lined with some kind of short black fur and they had a pattern of stars on the soles. He pulled them on – and they fitted perfectly. So these were Lyall's special boots – made for him and his circumstances. Glossy blue, fur-lined, star-soled, wall walking … wellington boots!

come and join the party

sue welford

N ow, no making any noise while we're out,' William's mum called from the hallway. 'Alison's got a lot of studying to do and she doesn't want to be disturbed. Finish that chapter of your book, then go to sleep, okay?'

William came out of his room and went to the top of the stairs. 'Okay, Mum.'

'And no getting your friends round, I know what you're like,' she added.

'No, Mum.'

'And no creeping down and watching sci-fi movies,' said Dad.

William leaned over the banisters. 'No, sir, Capt'n Kirk.'

Dad was putting on his overcoat, the big grey one that made him look like a bear. He fastened the buttons, then William's mum took his dad's scarf from its peg by the door. She wrapped it around his neck, tucking it in for warmth.

'There's plenty to eat if you fancy some supper, William,' said Mum. 'Some of that chicken we had yesterday. Make yourself a sandwich and Alison too, if she wants one.'

'Yes, Mum,' William said. He tried not to sound impatient. There was a brilliant sci-fi movie starting in ten minutes and if they didn't get going he'd miss the beginning.

'And if Dracula drops in there's a bottle of bull's blood in the sideboard.' Dad was joking as usual.

'James, for goodness sake! You'll give the boy nightmares,' said Mum. 'Alison's got the phone number if either of you want anything. We're only down the road.'

'Right,' William said.

'And *don't* bother your sister, okay?'

'Okay,' William said.

William's dad opened the front door. Swirls of snow blew in. The light from the porch lit up the flakes and made them look like a plague of white butterflies.

'Don't forget to lock up,' said Dad. 'January *is* the wolf month, you know!'

Mum gave him a shove. 'Honestly, James,' William could hear her saying as they went out into the snow. 'You'll scare that boy to death.'

William's dad was like that. Always kidding on about scary things. It was no wonder William's mum was worried he'd have nightmares. William remembered the time his dad fixed a black plastic bag to a fishing pole and flapped it around outside his bedroom window.

'Was that supposed to scare me or something?' William had said afterwards. He hadn't let on he'd hidden under the duvet. He had been quite convinced there was a huge bat outside trying to get in.

The front door slammed shut behind them. From the landing window, William saw his parents get into the Range Rover. Their footprints had already disappeared, covered with a layer of fresh snow. It was coming down thicker than ever. William gave a shiver of delight. He couldn't wait until morning. He and Dad would build the best snowman ever.

Dad started the engine and soon the car's headlights swept the drive. He backed out and drove slowly down the road. The storm swallowed up the red tail lights as if someone had switched them off.

William heaved a sigh of relief. He ran downstairs and picked up the phone. He dialled his friend Ashley's number.

'Can Ashley come over to watch TV?' he asked his friend's sister when she answered the phone. It was always more fun watching a movie with a friend. Then you could pretend to be the characters. You could have interstellar battles in the front room when it had finished.

'Sorry, Bill,' she said. William could hear loud rock music playing in the background. 'We've got our cousins staying. They couldn't come at Christmas so we're having a party now. Why don't you come here? Someone could come and fetch you if the roads aren't too bad.'

'Can't,' he said. 'Me and Alison have got to look after the house while Mum and Dad are out.'

He dialled another number.

'Hi, Melanie. Do you fancy coming over to watch the sci-fi movie?'

'Sorry,' Melanie said. 'I've got to babysit for next door. Anyway, I'd never get over in this weather.'

William tried a few more friends, but the lines were all busy. The fourth one rang for a minute or two, then the line seemed to go crazy, buzzing and crackling. William held the phone away from his ear. It didn't clear, so he gave up.

In the front room William put a couple of logs on the fire. He scanned the list of programmes.

'Great,' he said to Blackie the cat. Blackie was snoring on the rug in front of the fire. '*Strangers from Another Planet*. Just my cup of tea.'

Blackie uncurled. He yawned and stretched.

William glanced at his watch. There was just time to get his pyjamas on and fix himself a sandwich before it started. He had already worked it out. If he was in his nightclothes when Mum and Dad got back then he could nip upstairs quickly. He'd hear the car so he'd just run up and jump into bed, and they'd never know what he'd been up to. Alison wouldn't know either. In fact it was highly unlikely she'd come out of her room until morning. It had worked several times before so there was no reason why it shouldn't work again.

William ran back up to his room. He could hear his sister's stereo blaring out. How she could study with that row going on he didn't know.

At the top of the stairs, William turned. Crouched. He fired his imaginary stun-gun at the android from planet Zeta he pretended was chasing him. He yelled 'Wow!' and jumped up and down with glee when the android rolled back down and disappeared in a cloud of blue smoke.

William rummaged through the airing cupboard and came up with a pair of clean pyjamas, his favourites, the ones with Star Trek characters on. It would have been just his luck to find they'd been eaten by a red cloth-eating spider borne on solar winds and known to be invading the airing cupboards of Earth.

In the kitchen, William peered through the glass of the back door. It was still snowing. The garden and the field beyond were one huge blanket of white. In the distance, the sky was orange. It looked strange, eerie and much brighter than William had ever seen it look before. The snow-light must make it look like that: a horizon from another world. He shivered. The sooner he'd fixed his sandwich and was back by the fire, the better.

William settled down in front of the TV. Blackie came, sniffing the smell of chicken. He purred and rubbed himself against William's legs. He was always like that, ignoring everyone until they'd got food.

William tossed him a piece of crust then picked up the remote control. He pressed the ON button. Nothing happened. He shook it and tried again. It must have needed new batteries. He got up and turned the TV on at the set. There was a lot of flashing on the screen, a scratchy whizzing sound. Nothing else.

William muttered to himself. He sat down by the hearth waiting for the picture to clear. He was warm now, so warm he took off his dressing-gown. He felt suddenly sleepy. He'd be really annoyed if he dozed off and missed the movie altogether.

Outside, the bitter wind moaned around the eaves of the house. It howled like a pack of wild wolves. William was really glad *he* hadn't had to go out to a party on a night like this.

It was then that he heard a noise from the kitchen.

William held his breath. It was a kind of whispering, a shuffling, the sound of something scraping on the vinyl floor. Then he heard a chair being pulled back, the rattle of dishes, the hiss of fizz escaping from a can. Maybe Alison was getting herself some supper.

'Oh, no,' William whispered to Blackie. 'She's bound to have heard the TV as she went past the door.' He decided he'd better own up. Maybe she'd let him stay up if he promised not to be rude to her or Mike, her boyfriend, for a week … well, perhaps not a *week*, a couple of days might be all he could manage.

William got up and went towards the kitchen. Suddenly, Blackie gave a yowl. He shot past William and dived up the stairs at warp six, still screeching like a maniac. What on earth … ? But Blackie always was a crazy cat. Everyone knew that.

William thrust open the door. 'Allie, if you promise not to tell them –!'

There were four figures sitting round the table. They were surrounded by cans of Coke, a bowl of coleslaw, packets of biscuits and crisps. One had a huge spoonful of coleslaw halfway to its jaws. When they saw William they stopped stuffing food and drink into their mouths and stared at him. Their amber eyes were wide and curious.

'Hey, kid!' one said. 'Come and join the party.'

William gulped. There was no sign of his sister.

'Er … how … ?' he stammered.

'Hey!' said another one before William could get any more out. 'I like your pyjamas.' It stretched out a huge, hairy paw. William could see cola fizzing from its crimson jaws. Its eyes glowed amber in the light from the bulb above the table. It pointed. 'Mr Spock … yeah?'

William swallowed again. 'Er … yeah.'

'What's on the back?' The biggest of them got up and shuffled towards him. William took a step or two backwards. He felt a paw touch his shoulder. He tried as hard as he could not to be scared. 'Turn round, kid,' the creature insisted. 'Let's have a look.'

William turned round.

'Hey! The Star Ship Enterprise!'

The others fell about. They hooted and laughed, slapping their skinny, hairy thighs with the flat of their paws.

'What's your name, kid?' they asked.

'W … William,' William said.

They all grinned. Wide, Coke-dripping grins. One held its paw over its muzzle and spluttered. Bits of coleslaw shot out between its claws.

'It's not *that* funny,' William said indignantly.

The third creature stood up. 'It's a great name, kid. Don't take any notice of these creeps.' It began to prowl around the kitchen. It looked in cupboards, in the pantry. It took out a packet of dried kidney beans Mum used for chilli con carne. It shook them out all over the floor, then cocked its head at the rattling sound they made as they bounced around. It got a packet of White-O washing powder from under the sink. It ripped the top off, sniffed, then sneezed. It threw the packet down. A stream of white and blue speckled powder spread across the floor.

'Hey, kid,' it said. 'Come and sit down.' It wiped its paw across its nose. 'Got any other grub? We're starving.'

William started to back off. He didn't even want to *think* about what Mum would say when she saw the mess. And as for his sister … she'd go completely nuts.

'Hey, don't go,' the biggest one said.

'I … was just going to look in the fridge,' William stammered.

Big One waved its paw. 'Great, go ahead.'

William took out the chicken carcass. There wasn't much meat left but maybe …

He held it out. 'This?' he said. Then he got out a plate of corned beef covered in clingfilm. He held that out too.

The creatures howled and put their paws over their eyes.

'Yuk!' they cried. 'Gross.'

'Sorry, kid,' Big One said when it had recovered. 'We don't eat meat. What do you think we are? Barbarians?'

William hastily put the plates back. 'Er … sorry,' he stammered. 'It's pretty weird, uh … wolves not eating meat.'

'Yeah, well.' They all grinned at him. 'We're Weirdwolves from Wellandia. Wellandian Weirdwolves never eat meat.'

'Oh,' was all William could think of to say.

One of the Weirdwolves slunk from its seat. It put its arm round William. 'He couldn't have known that,' it said. 'Poor kid. We haven't even introduced ourselves, have we?'

The pack growled amongst themselves. Their red tongues lolled out, dripping.

'Sorry, kid,' they mumbled. 'No offence.'

William shrugged. He was getting used to them now. The cunning eyes, the slavering jaws. He guessed he looked just as funny to them as they did to him.

'That's okay,' William said. 'None taken.'

'About that grub, kid,' the Weirdwolf in the yellow jacket said. 'We're really starved. We ran out of nosh way back in the second galaxy.'

William went to the cupboard next to the cooker. 'How about this?' He held up a tin of creamed rice.

One of the Weirdwolves took it from him. It put the tin in its mouth, bit down hard, and let out a yell. 'Wow, how come you earth people eat *this* kind of stuff? You must have teeth like iron.'

William couldn't help laughing. He got the tin opener from the drawer and showed the Weirdwolves how to use it. Soon the table was covered with half-empty tins.

'Um, yummy.' The Weirdwolf in the green scarf licked round the inside of a tomato soup can then threw it on the floor. 'Got any more, kid?'

William shook his head. 'Nope, sorry. That's all there is.' He certainly would have a lot of clearing up to do when the visitors had gone.

The biggest Weirdwolf, the one in the red jacket, held out its long, hairy arm. 'Come on, tell us all about yourself, kid. Know Mr Spock, do you? I met him on Antares Five once. Nice chap. No sense of humour, though.' It took a mouthful of cornflakes and washed them down with slimline tonic.

'I don't actually *know* him.' William sat down next

to Red-jacket. He felt more relaxed now. Hardly scared at all. 'I've just seen him on TV,' he said.

'TV?' Yellow-jacket said.

'Yes,' William stared at him. 'Er … you don't know Luke Skywalker, I suppose?'

'Luke who?'

'Skywalker,' William said.

Red-jacket shook its hairy head. 'Never heard of the guy. Hey, you sure there's no more grub?'

'There's some Christmas cake left,' William said.

'Cool, man.' The smallest one's mouth began to water. Dribble fell amongst the mess on the table. 'Go get it, kid. I really fancy a bite.'

All the Weirdwolves threw back their heads and howled with laughter. But when William came back with the cake, they fell silent.

'Hey, what's this?' Red-jacket picked up one of the plastic reindeer from the top. 'And this?' It held Santa Claus between its clawed, grey, leathery fingers.

'It's Santa,' William explained.

'Do you *eat* this little guy?' Red-jacket put Santa in its mouth and bit down. It pulled a face and took Santa out of its jaws. 'Tastes gross.'

William explained.

'What is he?' Yellow-jacket was leering curiously at the little plastic model. 'Some kind of pixie? I've seen pixies on Gaglia Sixteen.'

'He ain't seen nothin' like those little guys on Gaglia. They don't wear black boots.' The smallest

Weirdwolf snatched the plastic Santa from the other one's fingers.

They began to quarrel amongst themselves, yowling and yipping, throwing a few punches here and there.

'Hey!' William had to shout to make himself heard. 'You're making enough noise to wake the dead!'

They stopped.

'Wake the dead?' Red-jacket frowned. 'Look, kid, you'd better sit down and tell us all about this strange planet of yours.'

It must have been almost one in the morning: sixteen cans of Coke, a bowl of coleslaw, ten packets of crisps, a tin of peaches, a jar of Marmite, a packet of muesli, a bag of raw oven chips, two bottles of slimline tonic, twenty baking size potatoes and a frozen family size deep-pan three-cheese pizza later that they said they'd got to go.

They all got up from the table, grunting and sighing.

'Don't worry, kid.' Red-jacket hugged William close to its hairy chest. 'We might end up in this neck of the woods some other night, huh? Got a bit lost in the storm, you see. Didn't mean to come here at all. Hey, why don't you come to Wellandia to visit us some time, huh?'

'I'd love to,' William said.

Red-jacket took something from its pocket. 'Can I

keep this, Willum?' It held up the plastic Santa. 'I've got a kid about your age back home. I'm sure he'd like to hear all those stories you told us about this little guy and his house on a north pole.'

William could see the Weirdwolf was trying not to laugh.

'Sure,' William said. 'No problem.' He felt sure Mum wouldn't mind. Especially as Santa hadn't looked quite the same since Red-jacket bit half his head off.

When they opened the back door, the snow danced in. They shivered, hugging their bright jackets round themselves. The smallest one pulled its brown woolly scarf up over its ears. When it turned to William, tears ran out of its amber eyes and down its long nose. It put its hand on William's shoulder.

'Nice knowing you, kid,' it sniffed.

William shook its paw. 'Nice knowing *you*,' he said. 'Remember me to Mr Spock.'

'Sure will. I'll tell him you were wearing his pyjamas.'

Yellow-jacket slapped him on the back. 'Better get some sleep, kid. You look tired out. Sorry if we kept you up.'

William watched them go down the path. At the gate they turned to wave goodbye. Then they loped away, the snow swallowing them up like the great, white jaws of a whale.

William wandered back into the front room and sat

down by the dying embers of the fire. The Weirdwolf had been right. He *was* tired. Maybe he'd just have a little sleep before he started clearing up the kitchen. It looked like a bomb had hit it. How he was ever going to explain things to Mum and Dad, he just didn't know. He supposed he could try to blame Alison but that wouldn't *really* be fair, would it?

When William woke up, the clock said half past one. He sat up quickly. The party, the mess! He leapt to his feet. Then, with a giggle, he sat back down. Of course! He'd been waiting for the TV to clear and he'd nodded off. What an idiot! A chance to see one of his favourite movies and he'd blown it. The Weirdwolves … the party, it had all been a dream.

Then suddenly William heard the sound of the car in the drive. The front door banged. It was too late to rush upstairs and pretend to be fast asleep. He'd just have to own up that was all.

Mum and Dad came in to the hall, stamping their feet on the mat. Dad was talking in a loud voice.

'No,' Dad was saying. 'No one knows *what* caused it. *Everything* got blacked out. There was some talk of a UFO landing in the valley, but you know how people imagine things.'

William came out of the front room looking sheepish. Mum was standing in the kitchen doorway with her hands on her hips. She turned, her face like thunder.

'William! What *have* you been up to?'

....

'Er ... what?' William peered through her bent arm. He stared, stunned. He tried to speak but his voice seemed to have disappeared.

Dad was looking over Mum's shoulder. 'Been having a party? I thought we told you not to have anyone in?'

'They just turned up,' William managed to say. 'I couldn't turn them away, not in this weather.'

'Well, I don't think much of their manners.' Dad picked up a couple of flattened soup tins and threw them into the bin. 'You'd better help clear up.' He looked outside. 'Snow's stopped now,' he said. 'How did your friends get here? Their parents must have had a four-wheel drive. They'd never have made it otherwise.'

William went to stand next to him. Mum had got the broom and started sweeping up the mess. She was muttering something under her breath. Something about kids taking things for granted and if you couldn't trust a seventeen-year-old to keep her brother out of mischief what could you do.

'I don't know how they got here, Dad.' William gazed out into the snow-covered garden.

'There weren't any tyre marks in the drive. Came in that UFO, did they?' said Dad with a grin.

William grinned back. 'Don't be silly, Dad,' he said. '*Now* who's imagining things.'

sponsored
hazel townson

Jack, are you deaf?' Alice Ray called to her husband. 'There's somebody at the door.'

Alice was upstairs dusting in one of the bedrooms, and she didn't see why she should have to trail downstairs again when Jack was in the kitchen.

Jack had certainly heard the doorbell but had chosen to ignore it. This was not a good moment. He was supposed to be cleaning out the waste-pipe under the sink but had come to a nasty blockage. He felt hot, tired and frustrated. His hands were filthy, his arms were streaked with muck up to the elbows and the smell was totally disgusting. It was hardly a state in which to be confronting callers.

All the same, at Alice's second shout he sighed and struggled to his feet. Grumbling under his breath, he wiped his hands defiantly on a clean tea-towel.

Jack reached the door in a mean mood and wrenched it open to find a blond boy, aged about ten, staring solemnly up at him.

'Well, what is it?'

'Please would you like to sponsor me …?' the boy began politely.

Jack gave a huge snort of disgust. Fancy dragging him to the door for a thing like that! Anyway, there was far too much of this nonsense going on. Sponsored walk; sponsored swim; sponsored fast; sponsored read; even sponsored silence – you name it, he'd supported it. Cost a fortune, it did.

He felt like slamming the door in the boy's face. But then he realised that this might well be one of his own children's friends – a classmate of Robert's or a brother of one of Emily's cronies. The lad was about their age.

Grudgingly, Jack took the proffered clip-board and scribbled his name where the boy showed him.

'Kids!' he was thinking, 'Always wanting something. Never satisfied, our two included!'

The boy checked the signature, then wandered off, apparently quite satisfied. Jack started back to the kitchen.

Alice leaned over the banister rail.

'Who was it, then?'

'Oh, only some kid wanting sponsoring. Blessed pests, they are.'

'Sponsoring for what?'

'I dunno!'

'Well, why didn't you ask?'

'He'll tell us when he comes for his money!'

Several days passed before the blond boy called again. This time he had a girl with him, equally blonde but slightly smaller than himself. The two of them were so alike that she must obviously be his sister, if not his twin.

Jack answered the door again, in a better mood this time. He recognised the boy at once.

'Oh, it's you!'

He began searching his pockets for some money.

'What's the damage, then?' he asked.

The boy gave Jack the full force of his solemn stare.

'No damage,' he replied politely, 'Unless you break the agreement, of course. It's up to you.'

'You what?'

Jack was outraged. He paused with his fist full of coins and scowled at the boy.

'Now, look here!' he said sternly, 'You can't go around talking to people like that. You'll end up in a lot of trouble …'

But before he could say any more the boy took hold of the girl's hand and began to draw her into the house. Together they pushed their way firmly past Jack and advanced down the hall towards the kitchen.

Jack could not believe his eyes.

'Where do you think you're going?'

The odd thing was that Jack suddenly felt afraid. Afraid of two young children, no older than his own pair! What was the matter with him? He should have stopped their progress, but he didn't. He simply stood there staring after them as they approached the kitchen.

Suddenly the kitchen door flew open and Alice's head appeared.

'Now what's going on?'

Alice had been baking lemon buns for her children

to eat with their glass of milk when they came in from school, and a warm, delicious smell spread through the hall.

'Oh – hello!' Alice was surprised to see the boy and girl, but assumed they must be friends of her children.

'Come to play, have you? You're a bit early. Robert and Emily aren't home yet. They'll be another quarter of an hour or so.'

Obviously these two went to a different school which finished earlier.

'I am Robert and this is Emily,' the boy announced solemnly in what Alice took to be a slightly foreign accent.

Alice giggled uneasily. 'Well, fancy that. There's a coincidence then.'

She stared in growing bewilderment at the two children, knowing quite well she had not seen them before. Nobody could forget such unusual features.

The girl pushed past Alice and began to walk round the kitchen, examining everything with great interest. At last she said, 'I think we shall like it here, Robert.'

'Of course we shall, Emily. It's what we've always wanted.' The boy walked over to the refrigerator and opened it, smiling at the contents.

The girl turned to Alice.

'No reason why we shouldn't get on. You will soon grow used to us.'

Then the boy sat down on Robert's chair and turned to Jack.

'It would have been quite in order for you just to sponsor me,' he said, 'but you wrote "2p" which we took to mean "two people", so I brought my sister along as well. Anyhow, it will be better this way, two of a kind under the same roof. We can work together. What is it you say? – two heads are better than one?'

Alice stared wildly at Jack. 'What are they on about?' She suddenly realised she felt deathly cold, despite her afternoon in the hot kitchen.

Wide-eyed, Jack slowly shook his head, unable to speak a word.

The girl now sat down in Emily's place at the kitchen table and reached for a bun, while the boy picked up Robert's glass and began drinking his milk.

At last Jack pulled himself together. In a voice that sounded strangely shrill he cried:

'Now look here, who the dickens do you think you are, marching into our kitchen as if you owned the place … ?'

Solemn as ever, the boy replied:

'But we do own the place. We belong here now. You did not give me time to explain when I first called. You seemed very eager to sign and be gone. But you must have realised what you were taking on. It was written in two languages on the form. We are YOUR children now. You sponsored us for a life on Earth.'

Alice gave a cry as her hand flew to her mouth.

'Jack … ?'

For a moment she stood rigid with horror. Then true panic took hold as she shrieked:

'Where are our two? Our Robert and Emily – where are they?'

Even as she spoke, there came a mighty rushing sound from the field behind the house and a circular silver object, dazzling and immense, spun off into space at almost the speed of light.

a world of difference

eric brown

S uzie N'Dah found the alien in Safeways, down
the frozen food aisle. She didn't know that the
alien was an alien at first. She thought it was a
girl, just like herself.

Kim Reed and a couple of her friends had chased
Suzie through the small market town, shouting that
they were going to beat her up.

Suzie ran like the wind. Her ice-skating practice had
improved her running, making her fit and fast. She
dashed into Safeways, hurried down an aisle, and hid
behind a stack of baked beans. When she peered
round the corner and through the window, she saw
the tall figure of Kim leading the others past the
supermarket and across the cobbled town square. She
sighed with relief. All day at school Kim had threat-
ened to get her, and at home time Suzie had run from
the classroom and never stopped.

It was Friday now. She had a whole weekend free
from Kim to look forward to.

Suzie walked down the aisle to the exit, and then
she saw the girl.

She was thin and pale, dressed in a dirty pink
jumper and jeans too small for her. What made Suzie
notice her was not her thin face or her poor clothing,
but what she was doing. The girl had her hands thrust
into the refrigerator, clutching a family-sized tub of

raspberry-ripple ice cream as if frozen in the process of lifting it out.

Suzie told herself that she should ignore the girl, walk past her and go home. But the girl looked ill. She was breathing deeply, and her face was covered in beads of sweat.

Suzie stopped beside her. 'Are you okay?'

The girl turned her head, slowly. She blinked her big blue eyes, staring at Suzie without a word. Suzie guessed that she was ten or eleven.

'I said, are you okay? You'll get frostbite if you don't let go.'

The girl just stared, her thin face sickly pale.

'What's your name?' Suzie asked. 'I haven't seen you around here before.'

The girl moved her lips, and a tiny voice said, 'Help me.'

The request alarmed Suzie. She looked around to see if anyone was watching.

'What's wrong with you?'

'I'm too hot. I need the cold. Help me!'

'You've got a temperature – a fever. Wait here. I'll go and get a doctor.'

'No!' the girl hissed. 'Not a doctor. I need a cold place, and then I will be okay.'

Suzie could not help laughing. 'Is that why you're holding the ice cream?'

The girl nodded. 'That is why I am holding the ice

cream,' she said. 'To lower my body temperature to that which I am more accustomed.'

Suzie blinked. The girl's speech became more complicated with every sentence she spoke. *Weird* …

'Who are you?' Suzie asked.

'My name is …' and the girl said a word that sounded like *Fay*. 'Please help me. I am too hot and am in danger of expiring –'

Expiring … The word sounded odd, coming from the mouth of the scruffy ten-year-old.

'Okay, Fay. Tell me where you live. I'll take you home.'

'You cannot take me home. That is impossible. I need conditions where the ambient temperature is close to zero. Then I will no longer be in danger. Can you help me?'

There was something seriously weird about the girl, her need for cold and her strange speech. Suzie wanted to back away, not get involved, but at the same time there was no doubting that Fay needed her help.

'*Please*,' said the girl.

'Okay,' Suzie said. 'I know somewhere. Come with me.'

Fay dropped the tub of ice-cream and followed Suzie from the supermarket, her short legs moving stiffly. Outside the automatic doors, Suzie grabbed Fay's sleeve.

'What?' Fay asked.

'Not so fast. Kim and her friends are after me. If they
see me now …'

Fay looked at her. 'You have enemies?'

'I've never thought of them as *enemies*,' Suzie said.
'But I suppose you could call them that.'

'Why do they wish you harm?'

Suzie scanned the cobbled square. There was no
sign of Kim or the others. She turned to Fay. 'Because
of this,' she said, pointing to her skin. 'They are white
and I'm black.'

Fay blinked. 'In this country people are antagonis-
tic towards others of difference?'

Suzie laughed. 'You could put it like that,' she said.
'Where have you been all your life? Come on, follow
me.'

They crossed town and headed for the skating rink.

'Don't be scared. Just go easy at first, okay? Hold onto
the rail until you feel confident enough to let go.'

She helped Fay onto the ice. The girl clutched the
rails and knelt, laying a palm flat on the surface of the
wet ice. An expression of bliss crossed her face. Suzie
was glad that there was no one else on the rink to
witness the girl's strange behaviour.

'Cold enough for you?' Suzie asked.

'For the time being, it will be okay. How long can I
remain in this building?'

'Well …'

Last year, after evening skating practice, Suzie had

fallen asleep in the seats overlooking the rink. She had awoken in darkness, wondering where she was. Then she'd remembered, and panicked. Luckily a security guard had heard her cries, found her and phoned her father.

'You can stay all night if you want,' Suzie said. 'I'll show you … if you tell me who you are and where you're from.'

Fay looked at her. 'I am from another country, a cold place –'

'The Arctic?'

The girl nodded.

'How did you get here?'

'How else? I flew.'

'Okay. Silly question.' Suzie shook her head, exasperated. 'Look, I'm not stupid. Even Eskimos don't like the cold like you do. They wear thick coats to protect themselves. You –' she looked at Fay's hands, flat on the ice – 'you seem to *need* the cold.'

The girl stared at Suzie, her big blue eyes unblinking, and then looked away.

Later, when Suzie had done a few practice laps, she took Fay into the darkened seats high above the rink. 'Stay here. Hide behind the seats. In a few hours they'll turn the lights out. Then you can go down to the ice again. I'll come and see you tomorrow, okay?'

Fay nodded.

Suzie stared at the girl in the shadows. In the hour she had been with Fay, the strange girl had changed.

She looked taller now, and not as thin. And – but surely Suzie was imagining this – her skin was no longer deathly pale, but almost bronzed.

She said a hurried goodbye to Fay and quickly left the building.

Suzie ate supper with her mother and father. The TV muttered in the corner of the room. 'You were late home tonight, Sue,' her mother said.

'I went to the rink.'

'I don't like you staying out so late.'

Suzie stared at her mother. 'I was *practising*. You go on about how I should always practise, and then when I do …'

Her father shushed them. 'Listen – news about the meteor.'

'What meteor?' Suzie asked.

'Listen, and you'll find out.' He turned up the sound.

Suzie watched the report. Last night a meteor had crashed to earth a mile outside town, landing in a farmer's field and setting fire to the crop of wheat. The pictures showed a blackened field, a deep crater cordoned off by tape, and police standing guard. The reporter said that several eye-witnesses had seen the fiery ball hurtling through the sky, and he went on to say that the authorities denied that the object was a UFO.

Suzie woke at eight in the morning, pulled on her black leggings and orange sweatshirt.

She remembered that it was Saturday – no school. She would go to the skating rink, meet Fay and this time find out the truth about the strange, cold-loving girl.

'Fay? Fay, where are you?'

Suzie carried her skates over her shoulder and walked up the aisle between the banked seats. There was no sign of the girl.

'Fay?' Suzie called, peering into the shadows. She wondered where Fay had disappeared to.

Suzie was about to go and practise her skating when she heard a small voice call from behind the highest row of seats.

'Suzie – I'm here.'

Suzie ran up the aisle, relieved that Fay was still here. 'I couldn't find you. I thought you'd gone.'

She came to a sudden halt on the top step, staring.

The girl was crouching behind a seat, curled into a ball and hugging her shins. Except … the girl was no longer Fay.

Suzie took a step backwards, her heart hammering in her chest.

'Who are you?'

'I'm Fay of course. Please, don't be alarmed.'

The girl rose to her feet and smiled, and Suzie almost fainted.

She remembered thinking yesterday that the girl had changed in the short time she had known her. Well, she had changed even more now. She was no longer a thin, pale girl. She was taller, and no longer skinny. Her clothing had changed, too: now she wore black leggings and an orange sweatshirt ...

But the greatest change was in the colour of her skin. Today the girl was black.

Suzie was staring at an exact copy of herself.

'Don't be frightened, Suzie. It really is me – Fay.'

'How ... how did you ... ?' Suzie stared. It was like looking into a mirror and seeing her reflection.

'We – my people – have the ability to change shape.'

It came to Suzie, then, in a sudden, dizzying rush. 'You ... That meteor – it *was* a spaceship!'

'I lost control on entry into the Earth's atmosphere. Engine malfunction. I had to abandon ship before it hit the ground. I came down in a life capsule on the edge of town. In order to pass among your people, I changed shape into the first person I saw – a young girl.'

Suzie shook her head, hardly able to believe what she was hearing. 'But ... but why change again – why change into me?'

'For protection. The people who run this place know you. This morning, when the rink opened, I went down and skated on the ice. No one asked who I was, what I was doing here. They thought I was you.'

Suzie's legs felt weak and she sank to the ground. 'I don't believe I'm really hearing this.'

Fay sat down beside her. Suzie realized that they must look like twins, sitting there side by side.

'I come from a planet many light years from Earth,' Fay said, 'a planet called Vallaria which orbits the star you know as Beta Hydri. My planet is cold, as cold as the Arctic here on Earth. To me, your country is too hot. The air burns my lungs. That is why I need the cold, the ice.'

'But why have you come to Earth?' Suzie asked.

'To explore,' the alien replied. 'I intended to land in an uninhabited region of Earth, so that I would not be discovered. Then I could gather samples of rock and flora, and then report back to my people. We have been coming to your planet for many hundreds of your years.'

'And you've never made yourself known to us?'

The alien smiled. It was a smile Suzie had seen many times before, in the mirror. 'My people decided long ago that we should not contact your people. You are ... you are still a young race. You are still angry and violent. We feared that you would be suspicious of our intentions, and try to find some way to harm us. In years to come, when you have grown as a race and dispensed with violence, then we will make ourselves known to you.'

Suzie stared at the alien, trying to take in all that it had said. 'If you can change shape at random,' she said, 'then what's your real shape? What do you look like normally?'

Fay shook her head. 'You would find me … ugly, repulsive to look at. I am too *different* –'

'Then you're not really a girl, like me?'

The alien smiled again. 'On Vallaria we do not have males and females. We are all one sex. And I am not young. By the reckoning of my people I am middle-aged. But by your reckoning I am almost one hundred years old.'

Suzie opened her mouth in amazement.

Fay said: 'Later today a rescue ship will come for me and take me away from here. I want you to know that you saved my life – what is wrong?'

Suzie was staring down at the entrance of the rink. Kim Reed and her friends were standing around, watching the people going to and from the ice. Kim had come here only once before on Saturday morning: she had waited for Suzie to finish her practice, and then found her and dragged her outside …

Fay touched her arm. 'Suzie, what is it?'

'They … those girls, down there.'

'They are your enemies, Suzie? They are the people who bully?'

Suzie nodded, fearing that Kim would look up and see her.

Fay took her arm. 'Get down. Hide behind the seat!'

Suzie ducked. 'What are you going to do?'

'Stay there and do not move.'

'Don't go near them, Fay. You don't know what they're like. They'll hurt you –'

Fay stared into Suzie's eyes. 'You saved my life, Suzie. Now I will do something for you.'

And before Suzie could protest, Fay set off and ran down the aisle towards Kim Reed and her friends.

Suzie peered over the back of the seat. Fay had said something to Kim and was walking slowly towards the exit. A second later Kim and the others gave chase. Suzie watched them leave the rink, a sick feeling in her stomach.

She recalled what Kim and her friends had done to her, the last time … She closed her eyes. She would rather not remember what had happened, back then.

She decided that she could not let the alien suffer what she had suffered. She stood and ran down the aisle.

She hurried from the building, dazzled by the bright morning sunlight. She looked left and right, up and down the street, but there was no sign of the alien and Kim. Desperate, she turned left and dodged among the shoppers, then stopped. She realised that it was hopeless. She had no chance of finding them now. She would return to the rink, sit on the steps and wait until Fay got back.

She waited for two hours, but the alien never turned up.

At midday she decided to go home. She would

come back later, and with luck Fay would have returned safely.

She left the rink and walked across town. She was thinking about Fay's icy homeworld, Vallaria, when she heard someone calling her name.

She turned and saw Kim Reed walking towards her. Suzie froze, her stomach heaving in panic.

Kim stopped, towering above Suzie. She was an ugly girl, who wore too much make-up to cover her spots. She was looking down at Suzie, an odd expression on her face.

'I've been thinking about what you told me,' Kim said quickly. She could hardly look Suzie in the eye, as if ashamed. 'You're right. What we were doing – it was wrong. We shouldn't have got you, just because you're different ...' She made an awkward gesture with her hands, obviously finding the apology difficult.

Suzie watched her without a word, wondering what the alien had said to Kim.

'Look,' Kim went on, 'anybody says they'll get you, just tell me. I'll make sure you're okay.'

Kim smiled at her, then turned and hurried away.

Suzie was almost home when someone shouted 'Suzie!' and she knew straight away who it was.

She turned. 'Fay?'

The alien, still looking like a reflection of Suzie,

stood at the corner of an alleyway, gesturing to her. She pulled Suzie between the buildings.

'I am leaving very soon. I wanted to say goodbye, and to thank you.'

'And I want to thank you. What did you say to Kim? I saw her just now.'

'I explained to her that what she was doing was wrong.'

Suzie laughed. 'And she listened to you – just like that?'

Fay smiled. 'Of course not. I had to … persuade her. Shape-changing is not my only ability. I entered her mind and made her see that what she had been doing was wrong. I made her experience how she would feel if people victimised her because of *her* differences …'

The alien reached out and took Suzie's hand. 'It was the least I could do, in return for your help.'

There was a sound from behind the alien. Suzie stared down the alley. From nowhere, filling what seconds earlier had been emptiness, a silver object like a cone appeared. A circular hole opened in the side of the thing, and a blast of icy air whistled out. Suzie hugged herself against the cold.

She looked back at Fay. The alien was changing shape before her very eyes. Fay's face altered, lost its black pigmentation. The orange sweatshirt slowly disappeared, along with the leggings.

The alien was turning green.

Suzie backed away. Fay – the alien – stood before

her, more like an upright frog than a human, its slick green skin glistening in the sunlight.

The alien held out its hand. 'Suzie, please do not be afraid. I am still me, after all. I am the creature you saved – only *different*.'

Overcoming her fear, telling herself that the alien's appearance did not matter, Suzie reached out and took its cold hand in hers.

'Thank you, Suzie,' Fay said, then turned and walked towards the silver object.

Suzie watched as Fay stepped into the spaceship. The circular hatch closed behind her, became again the silver surface of the cone. Then, as suddenly as the spaceship had appeared, it was gone.

Suzie felt a sudden stab of sadness. She wanted to shout at Fay to come back, to talk to her. There was so much she wanted to tell the alien, so much she wanted to share with her friend.

She wondered when the aliens would show themselves again, how long it might be before they judged the human race civilised enough to contact.

She looked up, into the cloudless summer sky. She told herself that she could see a bright silver speck, flying high.

'Goodbye, Fay,' Suzie N'Dah whispered, 'and thank you.'

dolphin story collections

chosen by **wendy cooling**

1 top secret

stories to keep you guessing by rachel anderson, andrew matthews, jean richardson, leon rosselson, hazel townson and jean ure

2 on the run

stories of growing up by melvin burgess, josephine feeney, alan gibbons, kate petty, chris powling and sue vyner

3 aliens to earth

stories of strange visitors by eric brown, douglas hill, helen johnson, hazel townson and sue welford

4 go for goal

soccer stories by alan brown, alan durant, alan gibbons, michael hardcastle and alan macdonald

5 wild and free

animal stories by rachel anderson, geoffrey malone, elizabeth pewsey, diana pullein-thompson, mary rayner and gordon snell

6 weird and wonderful

stories of the unexpected by richard brassey, john gatehouse, adèle geras, alison leonard, helen mccann and hazel townson

7 timewatch

stories of past and future by stephen bowkett, paul bright, alan macdonald, jean richardson, francesca simon and valerie thame

8 stars in your eyes

stories of hopes and dreams by karen hayes, geraldine kaye, jill parkin, jean richardson and jean ure

9 spine chillers

ghost stories by angela bull, marjorie darke, mal lewis jones, roger stevens, hazel townson and john west

10 bad dreams

horror stories by angela bull, john gatehouse, ann halam, colin pearce, jean richardson and sebastian vince